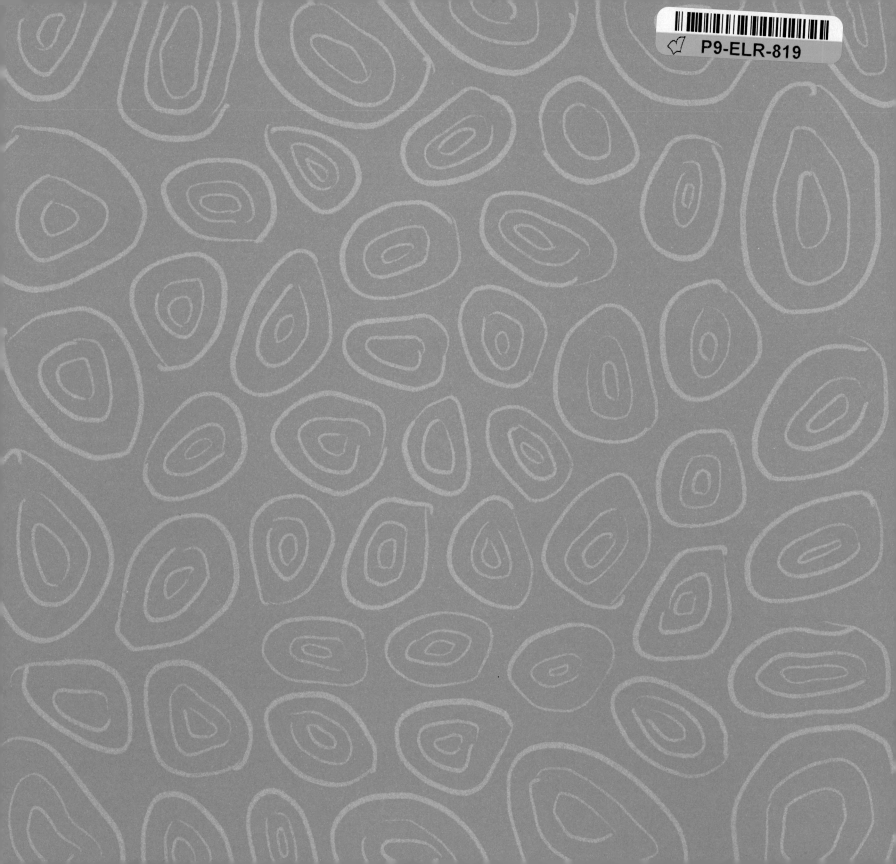

Truman

Written by **Jean Reidy**   Illustrated by **Lucy Ruth Cummins**

A Atheneum Books for Young Readers · New York · London · Toronto · Sydney · New Delhi
atheneum

TO HAGRID AND HIS SARAH—J. R.

FOR NATE—L. R. C.

ATHENEUM BOOKS FOR YOUNG READERS

An imprint of Simon & Schuster Children's Publishing Division

1230 Avenue of the Americas, New York, New York 10020

Text copyright © 2019 by Jean Reidy

Illustrations copyright © 2019 by Lucy Ruth Cummins

ATHENEUM BOOKS FOR YOUNG READERS is a registered trademark of Simon & Schuster, Inc.

Atheneum logo is a trademark of Simon & Schuster, Inc.

For information about special discounts for bulk purchases, please contact Simon & Schuster Special Sales at

1-866-506-1949 or business@simonandschuster.com.

The Simon & Schuster Speakers Bureau can bring authors to your live event. For more information or to book an

event, contact the Simon & Schuster Speakers Bureau at 1-866-248-3049 or visit our website at

www.simonspeakers.com.

The text for this book was set in Baskerville.

The illustrations for this book were rendered in gouache,

brush marker, charcoal, and colored pencil, and were finished digitally.

Manufactured in China

0420 SCP

6 8 10 9 7 5

Library of Congress Cataloging-in-Publication Data

Names: Reidy, Jean, author. | Cummins, Lucy Ruth, illustrator.

Title: Truman / Jean Reidy ; illustrated by Lucy Ruth Cummins.

Description: First edition. | New York : Atheneum Books for Young Readers, [2019]

Identifiers: LCCN 2017044780 (print) | LCCN 2017056183 (ebook) | ISBN 9781534416642 (hardcover) |

ISBN 9781534416659 (eBook)

Subjects: | CYAC: He may be slow but Truman the turtle is determined to find his girl Sarah, who has boarded a

city bus on her way to preschool. | Turtles—Fiction.

Classification: LCC PZ7.R273773 (ebook) | LCC PZ7.R273773 Tr 2019 (print) | DDC [E]—dc23

LC record available at https://lccn.loc.gov/2017044780

Truman was small,
the size of a donut—
a small donut—
and every bit as sweet.

He lived with his Sarah,
high above honking taxis
and growling trash trucks
and shrieking cars—

and the number 11 bus,
which traveled south.

Truman never honked
or growled
or shrieked
at anything
or anybody.

He was peaceful
and pensive,
just like his Sarah.

One day
Sarah ate a *big* banana with her breakfast,
clipped a blue bow in her hair,
and buttoned up a
brand
new
sweater.

She strapped on a backpack SOOOOOO big,
thirty-two small tortoises could ride along in it—

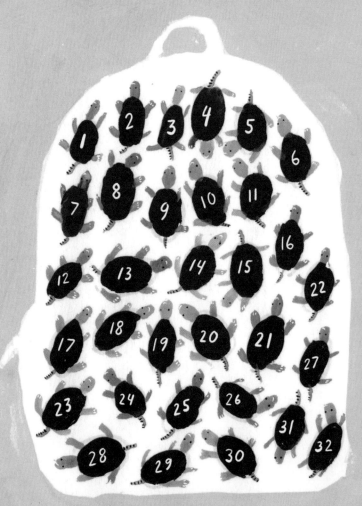

but zero tortoises did.

Sarah placed seven green beans in Truman's dish—

two more than usual!

She kissed her finger
and touched it to his shell
and whispered,

"Be brave."

Then she left.

Not to worry.
She'd left before.
And she'd always returned.

But this time

that backpack was
particularly big.

And Sarah looked
particularly pensive.

And that banana,

That's when Truman saw something
he'd
never
seen
before:

SEE NEW SIGHTS! HEAR NEW SOUNDS!
THINK NEW THOUGHTS!

Sarah boarding the
number 11 bus
going south.

The bus roared away.

Truman
waited for
Sarah to
return.

He waited.

And
waited.

He waited a thousand hours—tortoise hours, that is—

until he could wait no longer.

He would go after his Sarah.
He would catch the
    number 11 south.
Even amid the honking and
    the growling and the shrieking.

Even if it seemed . . .

That's when he noticed
the rocks—
three rocks—
that had always been there.

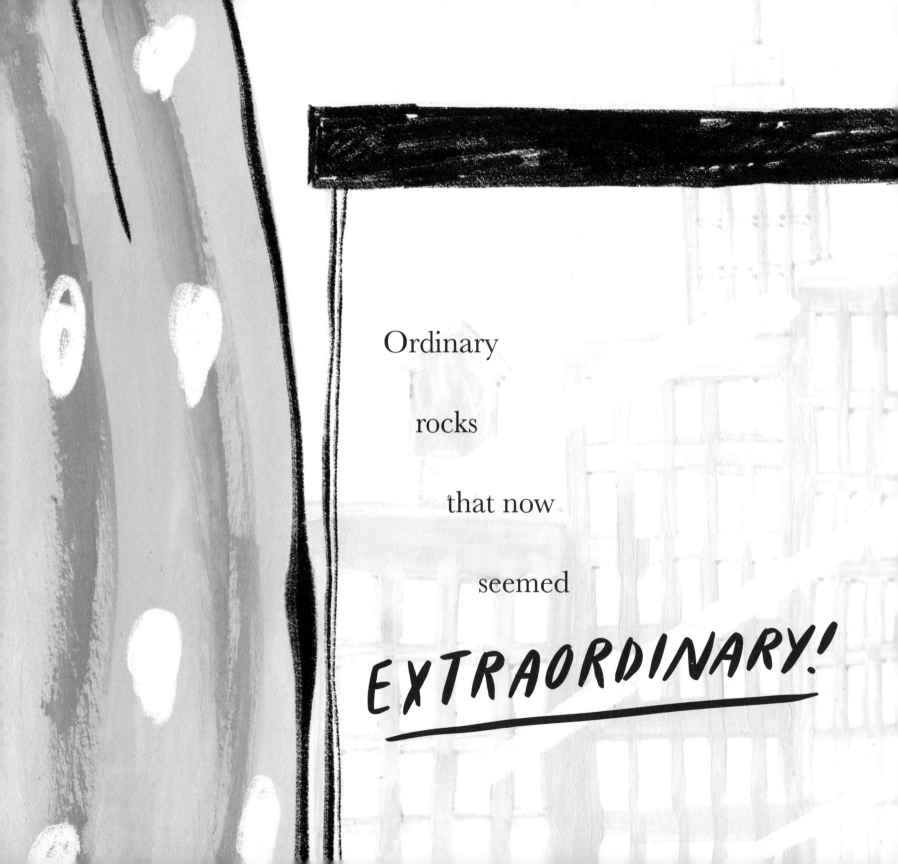

Ordinary

rocks

that now

seemed

EXTRAORDINARY!

And the arm of
the couch,

and the pillow
propped just right,

and that
tall, tall
boot.

And the rug!
That glorious . . .

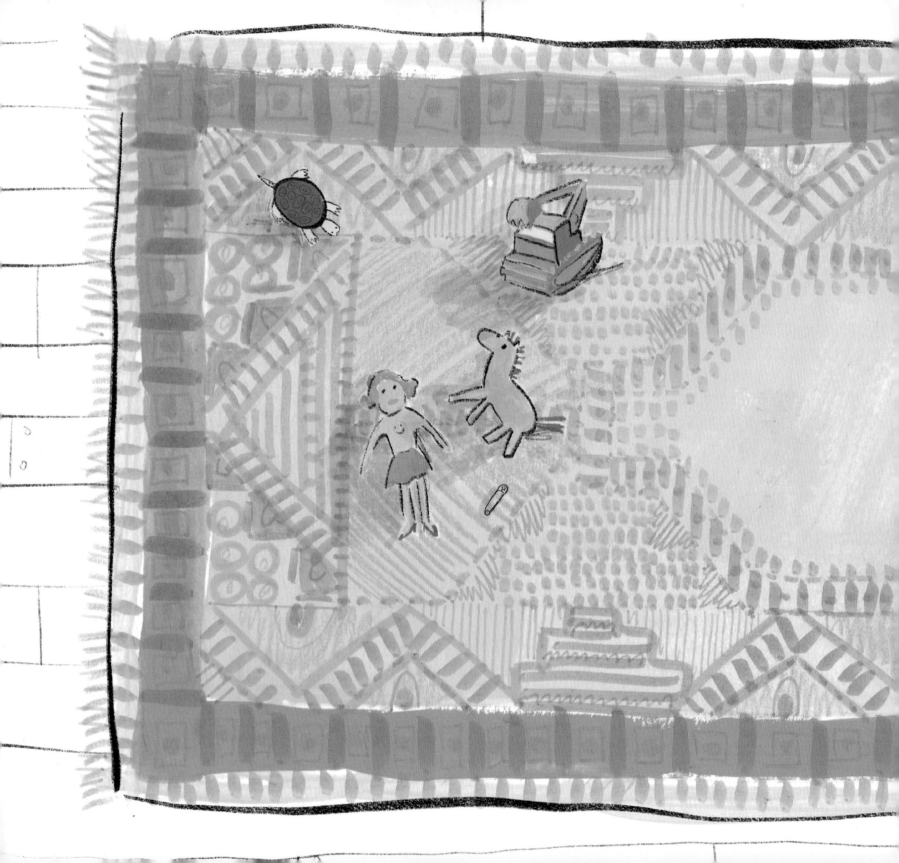

ENDLESS rug.

Without Sarah, their home seemed vast

and uncharted

and unsettling.

But perhaps *most* unsettling
was that Truman could no longer see
the taxis
or the trash trucks
or the cars

or the number
11 bus.

Which way was south anyway?!?!

Now the sun hung low,
like Truman's head

and heart.

Just then:

And then:

VROOM!
SCREECH!
WHISH!

Up floors and under
doors, Truman heard it.
A bus!

It was time.
Time to catch the
number 11 south.
Amid the honking and
the growling and the
shrieking.

Yet standing there
in that ray of light,
Truman felt peaceful and
pensive and . . .

BRAVE!

But just as he was about to
slip under the door,
through that opening barely
the size of a small tortoise . . .

SARAH!

She spotted him,
shining like the sun.

"Truman!" she cried.

She scooped him up
and said things like

"Oh, my goodness!"
and
"You!"
and
"How did you ever?"
and

Sarah kissed her finger
and touched it to his shell
and tucked him back safely in his tank,

where he was peaceful
and pensive and . . .

And later,
just before
bedtime, she
read him a
story.

Now Truman knew
that one day soon
he and his Sarah might travel south

to see new sights
and hear new sounds
and think new thoughts . . .

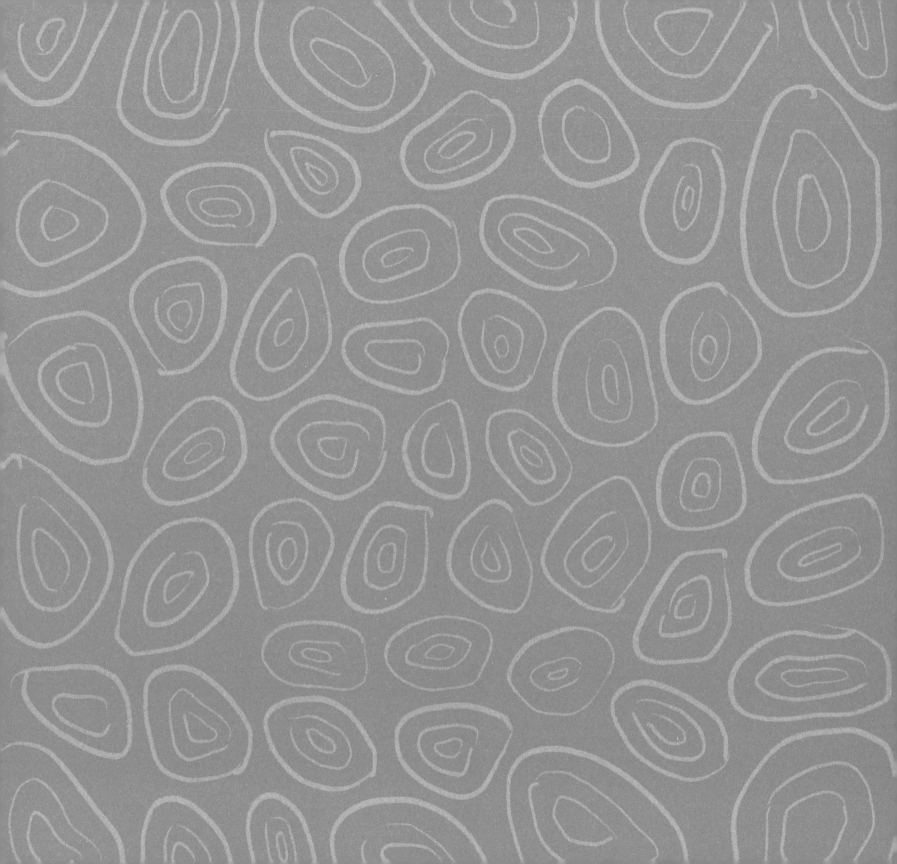